For Darcy & Keelan
xx

First published 2008 by Macmillan Children's Books, a division of Macmillan Publishers Limited. 20 New Wharf Road, London N1 9RR, Basingstoke and Oxford. Associated companies throughout the world. www.panmacmillan.com   ISBN: 978-0-230-01491-6   Text and illustrations copyright © Emily Gravett 2008. The right of Emily Gravett to be identified as the author and illustrator of this work has been asserted by her in accordance with the Copyright, Designs and Patents Act 1988. All rights reserved. No part of this publication may be reproduced, stored in or introduced into a retrieval system, or transmitted, in any form, or by any means (electronic, mechanical, photocopying, recording or otherwise) without the prior written permission of the publisher. Any person who does any unauthorized act in relation to this publication may be liable to criminal prosecution and civil claims for damages. A CIP catalogue record for this book is available from the British Library.

Printed in China. 9 8 7 6 5 4 3 2 1

The
Odd
Egg

Emily Gravett

Macmillan Children's Books

All the birds had laid an egg.

All except for Duck.

Then Duck found an egg!

He thought it was the most beautiful egg in the whole wide world.

But the other birds did not.

Then . . .

TWIT-TWO x 2 =

CHEEP!

Creak Crack

I'm a prettyoy!

Creak Crack

honk

honk

$-8 \times 26 + 6 + 6 \times b \times woo - Twoo + O \div O =$

Creak Crack

All the eggs had hatched.

All except for Duck's.

Duck waited for his egg to hatch.

He waited . . .

and waited . . .

and waited.

Until . . .

CREAK
CRACK

SNAP